Hansel
— AND —
Grettel

A PARRAGON BOOK

Published by
Parragon Books,
Unit 13–17, Avonbridge Trading Estate,
Atlantic Road, Avonmouth, Bristol BS11 9QD

Produced by
The Templar Company plc,
Pippbrook Mill, London Road, Dorking, Surrey RH4 1JE

Copyright © 1995 Parragon Book Service Limited

Designed by Mark Kingsley-Monks

Printed and bound in Italy

ISBN 0-75250-753-2

Hansel
— AND —
Grettel

Retold by Caroline Repchuk
Illustrated by Annabel Spenceley

|| •PARRAGON• ||

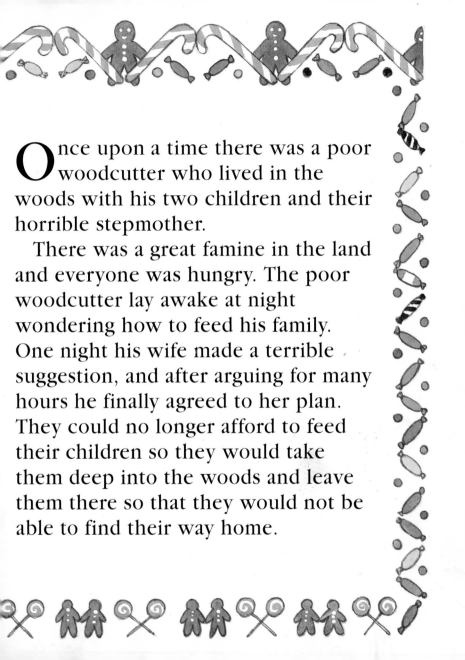

Once upon a time there was a poor woodcutter who lived in the woods with his two children and their horrible stepmother.

There was a great famine in the land and everyone was hungry. The poor woodcutter lay awake at night wondering how to feed his family. One night his wife made a terrible suggestion, and after arguing for many hours he finally agreed to her plan. They could no longer afford to feed their children so they would take them deep into the woods and leave them there so that they would not be able to find their way home.

Little did they know that the childr[en]
were awake in the room next door, an[d]
heard everything that was said. Grett[e]
wept bitterly, and her brother Hansel
comforted her. He had a plan.
Later that evening, he slipped
outside and filled his pockets
with white pebbles.

Next morning the family set off
early to the forest. Their father had
told the children that they were
going to chop wood.

The two unhappy children trailed behind their parents, but after every few steps, Hansel dropped a white pebble from his pocket onto the path.

When they reached the middle of the forest, their father lit a fire, then went away with their stepmother, promising to return later.

Hansel and Grettel ate the small piece of bread they had been given, then lay down by the fire and before long fell fast asleep.

When they awoke it was dark, and they were very frightened, but when the moon came out it lit up the trail of shining white pebbles so they were able to find their way home. Their stepmother pretended to be relieved to see them, and told them off for staying so late in the woods.

Their father was overjoyed, for he was ashamed of leaving them. But that night they overheard their parents arguing again. "The children must be got rid of or we'll all starve," said their stepmother. "We'll lead them deeper into the wood this time." Sadly their father was forced to give in.

Later Hansel tried to go outside and collect more pebbles, but this time the door was locked. By morning he had thought of another plan. This time as they headed into the forest, he crumbled his piece of bread in his pocket, and after every few steps he dropped a piece on the ground.

Their stepmother led them deep into the forest, farther than they had ever been before. Again their father lit a fire and then their parents left to go and chop wood, promising to return later.

Soon the children were fast asleep and awoke once more when it was dark. When the moon came up they searched for the path of breadcrumbs but, alas, they could not find any because the birds had eaten them all up. Try as they might they could not find their way back home.

The two poor children wandered about all night and day. They were tired, hungry and frightened, and felt sure they would die if help did not come soon.

Just then they saw a beautiful white bird on a branch.

The bird sang so sweetly that the children stopped and listened, then followed her as she flew on deep into the heart of the wood, until they came to a little cottage.

Drawing closer they saw that it was made of gingerbread! Its roof was made of honey cake and the windows were all of barley sugar!

"Now for a feast," said Hansel. "What a treat!" He broke off a piece of roof, and started to eat. It tasted of butter, sugar and honey. Grettel munched hungrily on a large piece of barley sugar window.

Suddenly the door opened and an old woman hobbled out. Hansel and Grettel were terrified and dropped their food. But the old woman smiled and invited them inside.

She made the children a lovely dinner of sweet honeyed pancakes, with apples and nuts. Then she tucked them into two beautiful white beds. They felt as if they were in heaven.

But the old woman who seemed so kind and friendly was really a witch! It was her white dove that had led them to the little house. She had built it all of gingerbread just to tempt children, and now she had two of them trapped! She planned to kill, cook and eat them — and make a real feast of it!

Next morning when the wicked witch saw the children sleeping peacefully she rubbed her hands and chortled, "That'll be a tasty morsel!"

She shook Hansel awake, carried him off to a small cage and locked him inside. Hansel screamed as loud as he could, but he could not escape.

Then the old witch woke Grettel and told her to cook for her brother.

"I want him nice and fat and then I'll eat him all up," she said.

Grettel began to cry, but it was no good, she had to do as she was told.

Every day the witch went to Hansel's cage and told him to hold his finger out, so she could feel if he was getting fat. Her eyesight was terrible, and she could not see that he always held out a bone for her to feel. She could not understand how he stayed so thin.

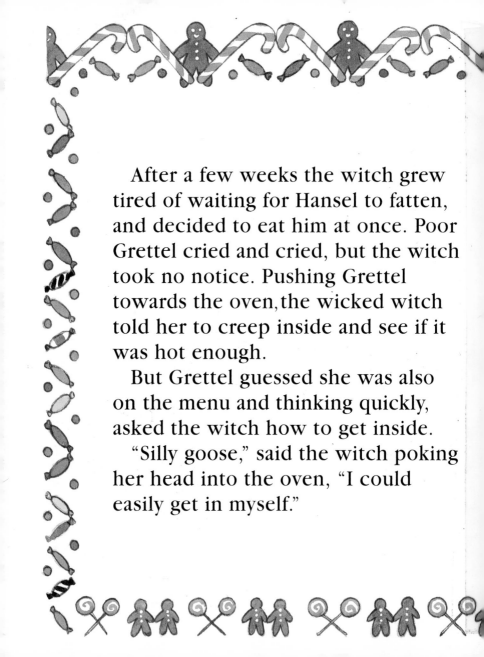

After a few weeks the witch grew tired of waiting for Hansel to fatten, and decided to eat him at once. Poor Grettel cried and cried, but the witch took no notice. Pushing Grettel towards the oven, the wicked witch told her to creep inside and see if it was hot enough.

But Grettel guessed she was also on the menu and thinking quickly, asked the witch how to get inside.

"Silly goose," said the witch poking her head into the oven, "I could easily get in myself."

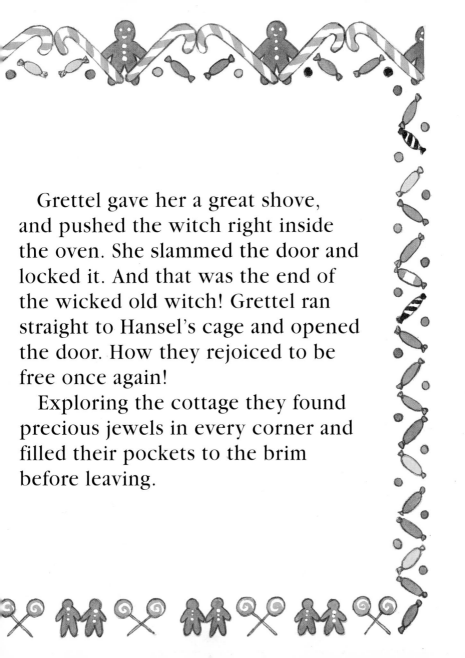

Grettel gave her a great shove, and pushed the witch right inside the oven. She slammed the door and locked it. And that was the end of the wicked old witch! Grettel ran straight to Hansel's cage and opened the door. How they rejoiced to be free once again!

Exploring the cottage they found precious jewels in every corner and filled their pockets to the brim before leaving.

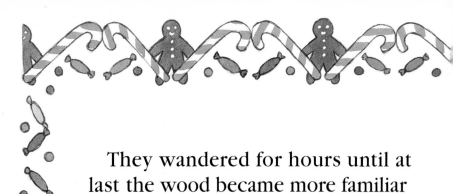

They wandered for hours until at last the wood became more familiar to them. Then in the distance they saw their father's house, and began to run. He was overjoyed to see them. He had been in misery since leaving them in the wood, and in that time their selfish stepmother had died.

They emptied out their pockets and precious jewels rolled all over the floor.

Their father hugged them and they all laughed for joy.

And so their troubles were ended and they all lived happily ever after.

JACOB AND WILHELM GRIMM

Jacob Grimm (1785-1863) and Wilhelm Grimm (1786-1859) lived in Germany and during their lifetimes gathered together over 200 folk tales to form the classic collection of stories commonly known as *Grimm's Fairy Tales.* *Hansel and Grettel* is one of the ancient stories they wanted to preserve and the Brothers Grimm retold it in such a way that it quickly became popular throughout Germany. *Grimm's Fairy Tales* are now known and loved throughout the world, having been translated into 70 different languages.